Rice Paper

Anna's Eighty-Eight

Owl

Common Bluebottle

Common Birdwing

Tailed Jay

Monarch

Pipevine Swallowtail

Ruddy Daggerwing

Hieroglyphic Flat

Moonlight Jewel

Lime

Mourning Cloak

Painted Jezebel

Zebra Swallowtail

Queen Alexandra's Birdwing

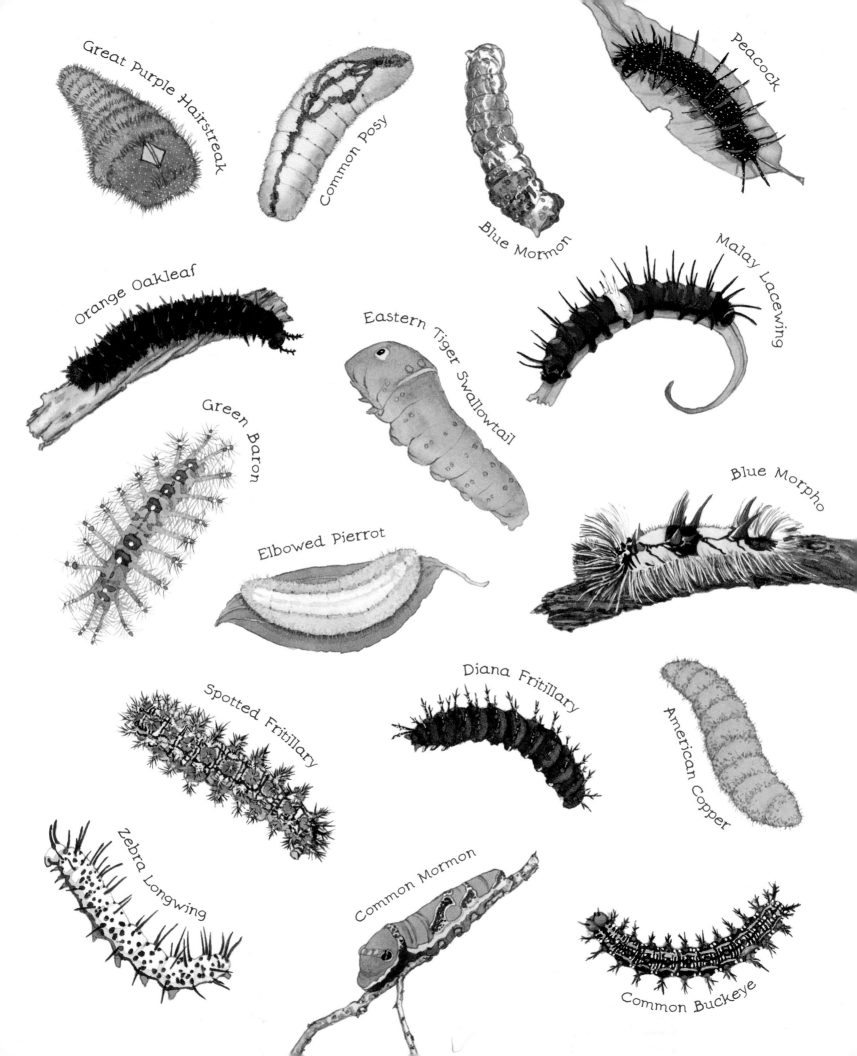

Great Purple Hairstreak

Common Posy

Blue Mormon

Peacock

Orange Oakleaf

Malay Lacewing

Eastern Tiger Swallowtail

Green Baron

Elbowed Pierrot

Blue Morpho

Spotted Fritillary

Diana Fritillary

American Copper

Zebra Longwing

Common Mormon

Common Buckeye

For my Sri Lankan friend and diviner of codes,
Dilshan Madawala. —D. A.

For my father—Frank J. Carlisle, Jr.—the blue-eyed
sailor, who is my source for all things wise and wonderful.
Among other things, he taught me the value of an interest
in the natural world and our place in it. —S. L.

Blue-Eyed Sailor

3 3113 03127 7389

ACKNOWLEDGMENTS:

Victoria Rock, editor, and Sara Gillingham, book designer,
for their wisdom and dedication to quality in children's books.

Jeffrey S. Pippen, Nicholas School of the Environment, Duke University; Nicky Davis, Wild Utah Project, Butterflies
and Moths; Linden Gledhill, photographer, Philadelphia, PA; Adrian Hoskins, LearnAboutButterflies.com, Hampshire,
England; Teh Su Phin, Panang Butterfly Farm, Malaysia; Lizanne Whiteley, Conservation of Butterflies in South Africa;
Robert N. Wiedenmann, Dept. of Entomology, University of Arkansas; Silvia Mecenero, South African Butterfly
Conservation Assessment; Steve Woodhall, President, Lepidopterists' Society of Africa; Jean-Claude Petit,
Butterflies of Sangau National Park, Ecuador; Niklas Wahlberg, Dept. of Biology, University of Turku, Finland;
André Victor Lucci Freitas, Universidade Estadual de Campinas, São Paulo, Brazil; Museum Victoria's Discovery
Centre, Victoria, Australia; Gareth S. Welsh, Butterfly World, Stockton-on-Tees, England; Thomas Neubauer,
ButterflyCorner.net, Germany; John J. Obrycki, Chair, Dept. of Entomology, University of Kentucky; Halmar Taschner,
South African Nursery Assoc.; Melani Hugo, Butterfly Garden at Ludwig's Rose Farm, Gauteng, South Africa;
Tim Loh, British Columbia, Canada

Library of Congress Cataloging-in-Publication Data
Aston, Dianna Hutts.
A butterfly is patient / by Dianna Aston ; illustrated by Sylvia Long.
p. cm.
ISBN 978-0-8118-6479-4
1. Butterflies—Juvenile literature. I. Long, Sylvia. II. Title.
QL544.2.A87 2011
595.78'9—dc22
2010008548

Book design by Sara Gillingham.
Handlettered by Anne Robin and Sylvia Long.
The illustrations in this book were rendered in watercolor.

Manufactured by Toppan Leefung, Da Ling Shan Town,
Dongguan, China, in January, 2011.

1 3 5 7 9 10 8 6 4 2

This product conforms to CPSIA 2008.

Chronicle Books LLC
680 Second Street, San Francisco, California 94107
www.chroniclekids.com

Southern Dogface

Spotted Fritillary

A Butterfly Is Patient

Dianna Hutts Aston   Sylvia Long

chronicle books·san francisco

A butterfly is patient.

Great Purple Hairstreak

It begins as an egg beneath an umbrella of leaves,
protected from rain, hidden from creatures that might
harm it . . . until the caterpillar inside chews free
from its egg-casing, tiny, wingless, hungry to grow.

A butterfly is creative.

A caterpillar feeds on leaves, eating so much that it must *molt*, or shed its skin, many times. It can grow up to 30,000 times larger than it was when it took its first bite.

1ST INSTAR

15 DAYS

3RD INSTAR

21 DAYS

5TH INSTAR

26 DAYS

PREPUPA

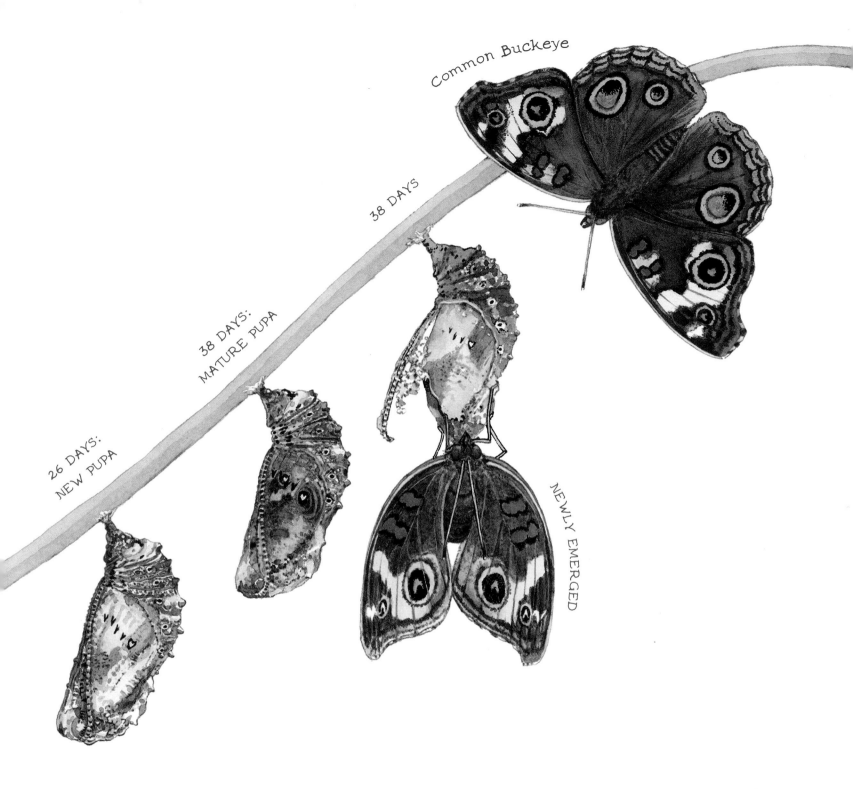

Common Buckeye

38 DAYS

38 DAYS: MATURE PUPA

26 DAYS: NEW PUPA

NEWLY EMERGED

Once a caterpillar has eaten all that it needs, it creates a protective covering called a *chrysalis*. Curled inside the chrysalis, it is growing wings. Now it is time for *metamorphosis*, changing from one form to another.

Zebra Longwing

Eastern Tiger Swallowtail

A butterfly is helpful.

Butterflies, like bees, help pollinate plants so that they can reproduce, or make seeds. As a butterfly flits from flower to flower, sipping nectar, tiny grains of pollen cling to its body, then fall away onto other flowers. Seeds are only produced when pollen is transferred between flowers of the same species. This is called *pollination*.

Owl

Peacock

A butterfly is protective.

Butterflies use their wings to protect themselves from predators such as hungry birds, lizards, and other insects. Some butterflies have markings on their wings called *eyespots*. Scientists don't know what they are used for—perhaps to scare away predators or attract mates!

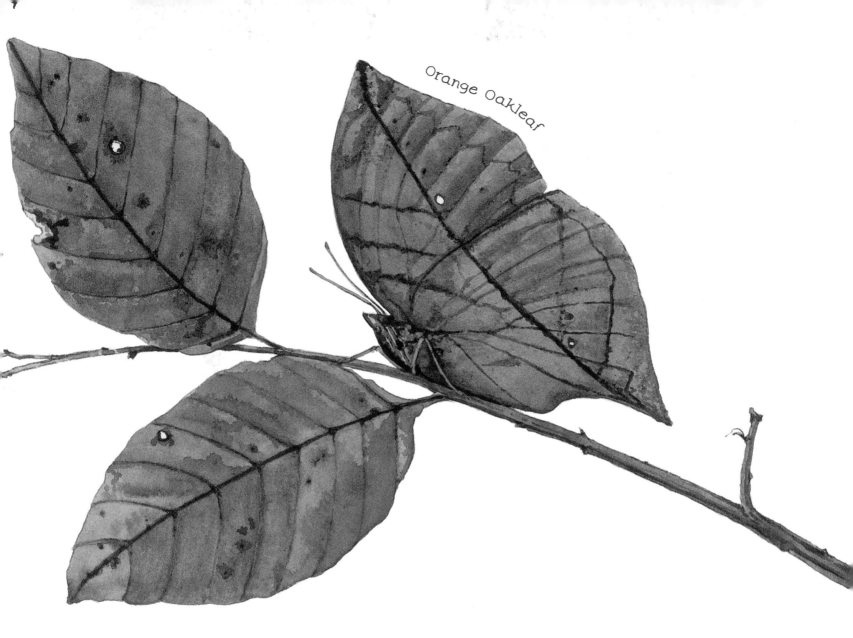

Orange Oakleaf

Wings can help butterflies *camouflage*,
or hide, themselves in the environment.
One kind of butterfly, the peacock butterfly,
makes a hissing sound by rubbing its
wings together when it is alarmed.

Pipevine Swallowtail

A butterfly is poisonous.

Monarch

The warning colors of some butterflies' wings—yellows, reds, oranges, whites, and blacks—tell predators that they are poisonous or bad-tasting. Monarchs and Pipevine Swallowtails eat poisonous plants as caterpillars so that they become poisonous as adults. Birds and other insects have learned not to eat them!

Moonlight Jewel

Painted Jezebel

Green Baron

Tailed Jay

Rice Paper

Common Birdwing

A butterfly is

Ruddy Daggerwing

Anna's Eighty-Eight

Elbowed Pierrot

Blue Morpho

Common Posy

spectacular!

Hieroglyphic Flat

Zebra Swallowtail

Spotted Fritillary

Malay Lacewing

Malay Lacewing

A butterfly is thirsty.

To find flowers, butterflies smell the air with their antennae. They taste with their feet but sip nectar, the sweet liquid produced by many flowers, with a *proboscis*, a "tongue" that coils and uncoils.

Lime

Common Bluebottle

Common Mormon

Blue Mormon

Some butterflies get their nourishment from rotting fruit
(*Blue Morpho*) or minerals. Often, a kaleidoscope of
butterflies gathers as a "puddle club" in mud near a pond
or a lake to drink water rich in salts and minerals.

A butterfly is big . . .

The rare Queen Alexandra's Birdwing is the largest butterfly in the world, with wings that can span up to 1 foot (30.4 cm). It lives in the rain forest in northern Papua New Guinea.

Queen Alexandra's Birdwing

Arian Small Blue

and tiny.

The smallest is the rarely-seen Arian Small Blue found
in Afghanistan with a wingspan of less than one third of
an inch (8 mm), about the length of a grain of rice.

A butterfly is scaly.

A rainbow of shiny, powdery scales covers the
wings of a butterfly, scales stacked like shingles on
a roof. Without scales, its wings would be as
transparent as the wings of a bee or a dragonfly.

The colors, patterns, and shapes of a butterfly's wings have a purpose. Some use their pattern of colors to attract mates. In places where the climate is cool, dark scales absorb heat from the sun, warming the butterfly's flight muscles. Butterflies are cold-blooded and must have a body temperature of 86 degrees F (30 degrees C) to fly.

Diana Fritillary

Mourning Cloak

Zebra Longwing

A butterfly

American Copper

Butterflies and moths belong to the same
family of insects, the *Lepidoptera*, which means
"scale wing." They are the only insects with
scaly wings, but there are differences between them.

Io

Cecropia

is not a moth!

Luna

Moths appeared on Earth between 100 and 190 million years ago, butterflies 40 million years ago, during the Cretaceous period, when flowering plants—and the nectar most butterflies need to survive—evolved. Nearly every kind of butterfly flies during the day, while most moths fly at night. A moth spins a cocoon made of silk, while a butterfly wraps itself in a chrysalis or exoskeleton made from its skin.

A butterfly

is a traveller.

Most butterflies, such as the Red Admiral or the Common Buckeye, migrate a short distance to find a warmer place, but some, like the Monarch, travel far. Although Monarchs weigh only as much as a few rose petals, they can fly almost 3,000 miles (4,828 km), from Canada to their winter home in Mexico, at a rate of 20 miles (30 km) per hour. Glider pilots have reported seeing Monarchs flying at an altitude of 11,000 feet (3,352.8 m)—higher than some clouds!

Monarchs

A butterfly is magical.

Monarchs gather in huge numbers in the
forests of Central Mexico waiting for spring.
Then they fly north, to the milkweed plants
in North America, where they lay their eggs.
Now it is time again for their metamorphosis.

Monarch

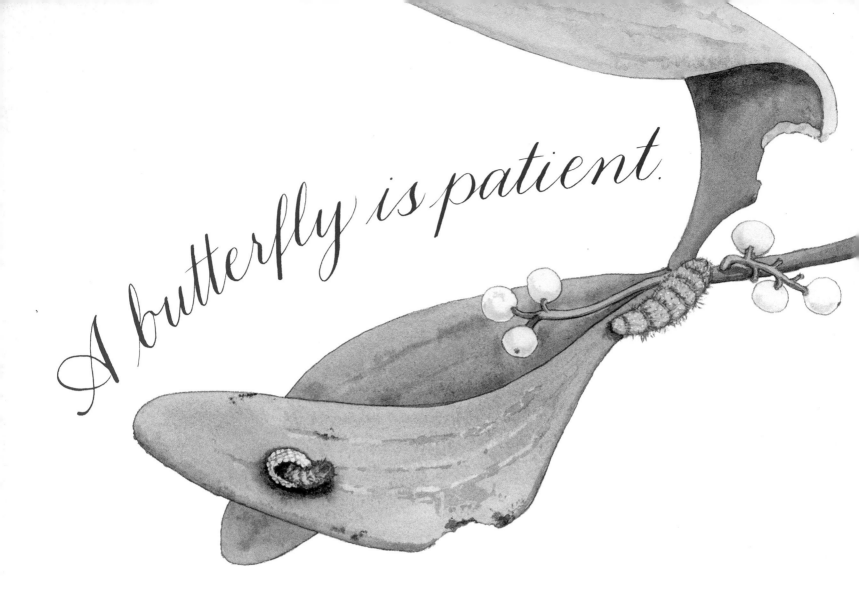

A butterfly is patient.

The egg hatches,
the caterpillar emerges,
feasting on leaves
before it wraps itself
into its warm,
protective chrysalis,

patiently waiting . . .

Great Purple Hairstreak

Great Purple Hairstreak

to soar!

American Copper

Arian Small Blue

Blue Morpho

Great Purple Hairstreak

Green Baron

Common Posy

Queen Alexandra's Birdwing

Blue Mormon

Rice Paper

Common Mormon

Common Bluebottle

Common Buckeye

Eastern Tiger Swallowtail

Ruddy Daggerwing

Elbowed Pierrot

Spotted Fritillary

Malay Lacewing

Owl

Orange Oakleaf

Pipevine   Swallowtail

Peacock

Zebra Swallowtail

Monarch

Zebra Longwing

Moonlight Jewel

Common Birdwing

Mourning Cloak

Anna's Eighty-Eight

Satyr

Hieroglyphic Flat

Diana Fritillary

Lime

Painted Jezebel

Tailed Jay